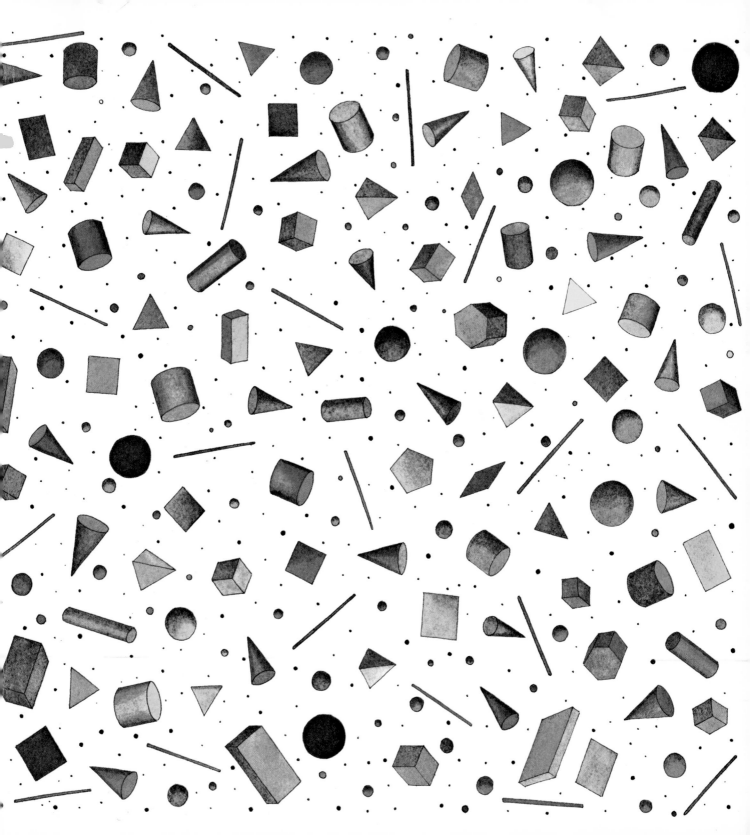

For Charlotte

First published in the United States 1983 by
Dial Books for Young Readers
A Division of E. P. Dutton, Inc.
2 Park Avenue
New York, New York 10016
Published in Great Britain by Andersen Press Ltd.

Printed in Italy
Design by Atha Tehon

Library of Congress Cataloging in Publication Data
Testa, Fulvio.
If you look around you.
Summary: Geometric shapes are depicted
in scenes of children in- and out-of-doors. 3/87
1. Geometry — Juvenile literature. [1. Geometry.] I. Title.
QA447.T47 1983   516.2'15   83-5310
ISBN 0-8037-0003-2

First Edition
(US)
10 9 8 7 6 5 4 3 2 1

J
516.2
TES

The art for each picture consists of an ink
and dye painting that is camera-separated
and reproduced in full color.

If You Look Around You
FULVIO TESTA

Dial Books for Young Readers

E. P. DUTTON, INC. *New York*

A point is the first star in the sky when night comes.

Two points are Charlotte and her dog running in the fields.

A line is the dog's leash.

A triangle is a brush, a pencil, and a ruler lying on my table.

A circle is what you see in the water
after you drop a stone.

A square is the magician's handkerchief.

A cylinder is Teddy Bear's drum.

A cone is what is left after you eat your ice cream.

A cube is what you use to play dice.

A sphere is a ball.

Our world is a sphere too.

And from far, far away it looks just like a point.